Stay Up Late

pictures by Maira Kalman

from a song by David Byrne

Puffin Books

For Mr. and Mrs. Kapishkin
and Mr. Tibor
in this whole world.
M.K.

PUFFIN BOOKS
Published by the Penguin Group
Viking Penguin, a division of Penguin Books USA Inc.,
40 West 23rd Street, New York, New York 10010, U.S.A.
Penguin Books Ltd, 27 Wrights Lane, London W8 5TZ, England
Penguin Books Australia Ltd, Ringwood, Victoria, Australia
Penguin Books Canada Ltd, 2801 John Street, Markham, Ontario, Canada L3R 1B4
Penguin Books (N.Z.) Ltd, 182–190 Wairau Road, Auckland 10, New Zealand

Penguin Books Ltd, Registered Offices: Harmondsworth, Middlesex, England

First published in the United States of America by Viking Penguin,
a division of Penguin Books USA Inc. 1987
Published in Picture Puffins 1989
1 3 5 7 9 10 8 6 4 2
Text copyright © Index Music, Inc. and Bleu Disque Music Co., Inc., 1985
Illustrations copyright © Maira Kalman, 1987
All rights reserved

This book is based on the song "Stay Up Late"
from the Talking Heads album *Little Creatures* on Sire records, cassettes, and CD's.

LIBRARY OF CONGRESS CATALOGING-IN-PUBLICATION DATA
Kalman, Maira.   Stay up late / pictures by Maira Kalman ;
from a song by David Byrne.   p.   cm.
Summary: Family members and friends entertain a new baby on his
first night at home.
ISBN (invalid) 0-01-400791-4
[1. Babies—Fiction. 2. Family life—Fiction.]
I. Byrne, David, 1952– . II. Title.
PZ7.K1256St 1989   [E]—dc20   89-32422

Printed in Japan by Dai Nippon Printing Co. Ltd.
Set in Bodoni

This book is based on the song "Stay Up Late"
from the Talking Heads album *Little Creatures*
on Sire records, cassettes, and CD's.

When I was a kid the whole
family would join my little sister and we'd
all eat baby food.

When I was younger I would
sometimes be mean to my little sister.
And sometimes she would get me back.
Now we get along fine,
in fact she lives next door.
(I turn on the stereo real loud and
blast it into her window.)

When I was a kid,
my little sister and I would sneak
out of the house without
any clothes on and
go sit on the neighbor's steps.

When I was a kid my little sister would
cover herself with stamps.

David Byrne

**Mommy had
a little baby.**

There he is
fast asleep.

He's just
a little plaything.

Why not
wake him up?

Cute, cute,
little baby.

Little pee pee,
little toes.

Now he's
coming to me.

Crawl across
the kitchen floor.

**Baby, baby,
please let me hold him.**

I want to make him
stay up all night.

Sister, sister,
he's just a plaything.

We want to make him
stay up all night.

See him drink
from a bottle.

See him eat
from a plate.

Cute, cute,
as a button.

**Don't you want to make him
stay up late?**

And we're having fun
with no money.

**Little smile
on his face.**

**Don't you love
the little baby.**

**Don't you want to make him
stay up late?**

Baby, baby,
please let me hold him.
I want to make him
stay up all night.

Sister, sister,
he's just a plaything.
We want to make him
stay up all night.

Why don't
we pretend.
There you go,
little man.

Cute, cute,
why not.
Late at night
wake him up.

Here we go
all night long.
With the television on.

Little baby goes "$\mathcal{Wooo}$"
all night long.

And he
looks so cute.

In his
little red suit.

All night long.

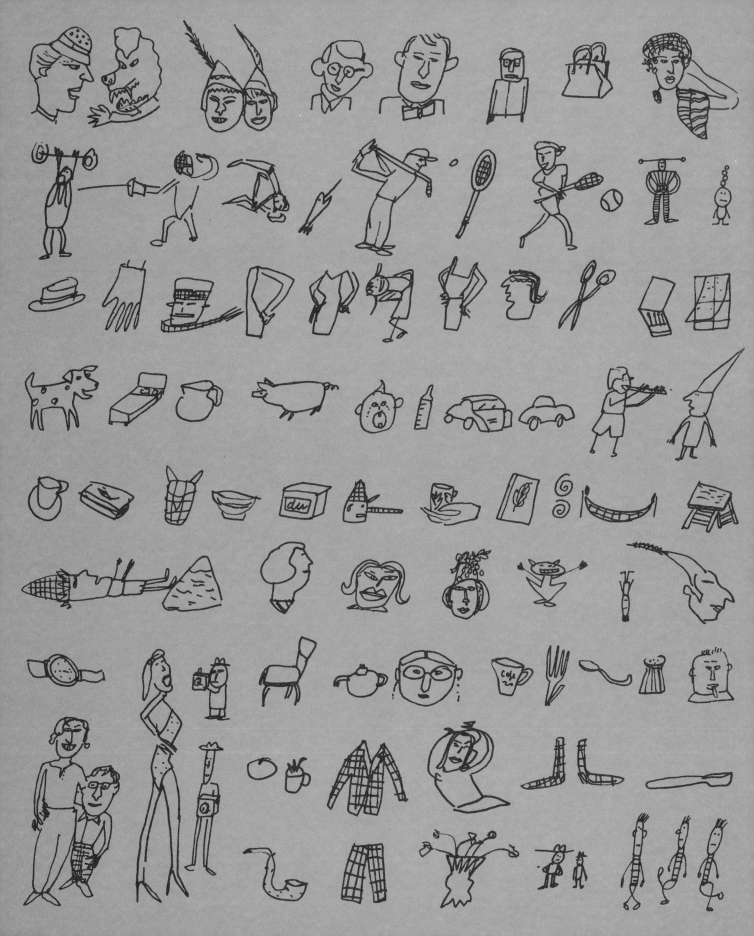